Marly

Marly

A NOVELLA IN ONE VOICE

Peter Gould

GREEN WRITERS PRESS

Brattleboro, Vermont

Printed in the United States

10 9 8 7 6 5 4 3 2 1

Green Writers Press is a Vermont-based publisher whose
mission is to spread a message of hope and renewal through
the words and images we publish. Throughout we will ad-
here to our commitment to preserving and protecting the
natural resources of the earth. To that end, a percentage
of our proceeds will be donated to environmental activist
groups. Green Writers Press gratefully acknowledges support
from individual donors, friends, and readers to help support
the environment and our publishing initiative.

Giving Voice to Writers & Artists Who Will Make the World a Better Place
Green Writers Press | Brattleboro, Vermont
www.greenwriterspress.com

ISBN: 978-0-9961357-1-9

For more information, visit the author's website:
www.petergouldvermont.com

PRINTED ON PAPER WITH PULP THAT COMES FROM FSC-CERTIFIED FORESTS,
MANAGED FORESTS THAT GUARANTEE RESPONSIBLE ENVIRONMENTAL, SOCIAL, AND
ECONOMIC PRACTICES BY LIGHTNING SOURCE. ALL WOOD PRODUCT COMPONENTS
USED IN BLACK & WHITE, STANDARD COLOR, OR SELECT COLOR PAPERBACK BOOKS,
UTILIZING EITHER CREAM OR WHITE BOOKBLOCK PAPER, THAT ARE
MANUFACTURED IN THE LAVERGNE, TENNESSEE PRODUCTION CENTER ARE
SUSTAINABLE FORESTRY INITIATIVE® (SFI®) CERTIFIED SOURCING

A few words before you begin

On the third day of the Wildbranch Environmental Writing Workshop in June 2011, our teacher Sandra Steingraber said, "Okay. Too much about cancer and toxic tap water, and what goes into our hot dogs. Tonight, try to write light-hearted. Write something funny, if you can."

It wasn't easy. The subjects that came up in class weren't funny. Our little earnest group had a worried, wounded pall that needed to be lifted. We were all in awe of Sandra; we wanted to be as righteous and heroic as she is.

That evening, while I sat outside the Sterling College Library in Vermont's north woods, this story popped into my head. The character and voice came to me entire—not a phenomenon I'm used to, and certainly not a voice I'd ever heard before. He started beating around my head like a bat at sundown. He kept coming back again and again in the weeks to come.

The literary form arrived at the same time. Never saw anything like it before. (That doesn't mean someone else hasn't tried it. Not claiming that.)

My advice to the reader? Get comfortable, pour yourself a local beer, and read the whole thing out loud. Choose a name and an appropriate voice for the guy. You'll have to fill in everything she says, and wait while she says it, but there's nothing intrinsically wrong with an interactive book, is there?

Right. That's what I thought, too.

PETER GOULD
March 2015

Marly

1

Hello.

I said HELLO. Just—I didn't mean anything by it. Where I come from, that's what you say when—

That's better. You from around here? Wait. I know you are.

You've just, got that look.

Okay, from the ground up. Nice hiking boots.

Really? Sustainable-harvest rubber. How cool is that?

Well, yeah it's important. Cause you wouldn't wanna tap out those trees in Brazil. Course they'll all be under Hydro Zingu next year. Can't stop progress.

Yep. Cruelty Free. Nice. When you're squishing all those newts and stuff.

Man-made uppers? No thanks, I don't do that anymore. Quit last week.

Just kidding. You want some beef jerky?

Oh. No problem. You don't mind if I . . . ?

Cool.

. . .

This is a neat place, huh?

No, the college. Middle of freaking North Nowhere. You seen their promo?

Yeah I actually did. Forty years ago, there's this defunct prep school, way deep in the woods, they hack the bushes away, they paint it white, turn it into Tree Hug U, and now they get people to pay forty thousand bucks a year to come up and take "watershed studies," "fluvial geomorphology," "chainsaw hi-jinx—"

Oh. You did? Oh.

No, it's all good. You did what you wanted to do. Did you like it?

Cool.

No, I'm not actually ENROLLED. I'm doing, you know, professional development. For my job. I'm in a class here. For a week.

Environmental writing. Save the planet. Not that it needs to be. The class looked interesting though. Paid my ten bills and hauled ass up here. WAY up here.

It's good. Well. It's pretty good.

Yeah, I'm learning stuff. But then this morning, our teacher says, "Write something funny."

Yeah. She says, "Funny *works*. If you can make people laugh, you'll get them to listen." That's easy for her to say. She's a full-time gag writer for the Upstate New York Anti-Fracking Coalition. If that's not a natural gas, I don't know what is.

Yeah I know. That was REALLY corny. I can't help it. I get this federal subsidy—ten percent of my jokes have to be pure corn.

Yeah, that was another one. I guess the percentage went up. I ain't no FOSSIL FOOL!

Hey do that again! Did you know you are REALLY pretty when you groan?

Sorry. I know. My dad was the same way. I mean, mom says he was. He—

Do? What do I do where?

Oh. Real life. Like when I'm not here?

I do P.R. For power companies. Host parties, hand out swag. Stage fake rallies. Get people comfortable with really bad shit, like, you know, eminent domain, forty-story wind turbines out the kitchen window, a little radioactivity, occasional earthquake, tap water catchin' fire. . . . Hey you want a free T-shirt? All cotton, I promise. You'd look great in a—

I don't know. I didn't look at the label. And you know, unions are not what they used to be.

OK, maybe later. I got lots—hey look, you see that girl walking around scowling? And that dude over there, with the frown?

Yeah they're in the class too. Funny doesn't

come easy. For some people it doesn't COME at all. Hey, doesn't that happen with a lot of WOMEN?

Sorry.

No, I know. Really Bad Joke. You're totally right. I just, probably, never NOTICED it. I'll pay more attention next time.

Hey now that was NOT nice.

. . .

The point is, if I could write something funny I wouldn't even be here. I'd have a job in TV. And anyway, the Environment is NOT funny.

No, well, actually, I take that back. We've been having some laughs lately. Half of Pakistan got flash-flooded. Serves 'em right for sheltering Osama. Russia got baked in an oven. Biggest oil spill in U.S. history, way to go, BP. We had the Mother of all Tornados, people scuba diving in the New York City subway, and not to mention, can you say Fukushima Dai-ichi?

I know. That wasn't actually man-made. And those Japanese. They were SO GOOD about it. They're not like us. Didn't even loot. Bunch of wimps. Always standing in line. They leave you these care packages on the doorstep. But, I ask you, who was the genius that put six reactors butt-up against the North Pacific Plate, and told them, okay, all ready, hit the switch–

I know. I should be more sensitive.

I'm working on it. Hey, speaking of that, you

want to meditate with me? Find a screened-in porch—

No. That's fine. It really is. We all have our personal dharma practice. *Om tot sot.*

. . .

So, uh, stop me if you heard this one. A polar bear and a spotted owl go into a bar—

Okay. See? I can stop.

How many environmentalists does it take to screw in a light bulb?

None. They don't BELIEVE in light bulbs. They don't want YOU to HAVE light bulbs. They want you to stay in one place and live in the dark. Look, there's one of them now, up in that jet plane flying to Chicago to make a speech.

Yeah, but don't worry. It's powered by methane from composted worker-owned vegan restaurant trash.

The black smoke? I don't know, there's probably some grease in it, organic canola oil, can't hurt ya, plus it's windy. That'll disperse the contrail.

CONTRAIL. That's that stuff hanging around after a jet flies over.

I know. I read that. You should NEVER EVER fly. Cause "Jet exhaust modifies the chemistry of the troposphere, reduces the terrestrial energy loss, adding to global warming." You think I didn't know that shit? That's why I ride my bike. Or, I used to. My wife took it when she—forget it.

Anyway, not to worry. NASA and the DOE are co-sponsoring a study on the impact jet fuel has on climate. The report's due out in January 2018.

I KNOW! We CAN'T wait. That's why Vermont's THE PLACE. You don't waste time doing studies.

Quick local solutions, that's right. What'd I say? Air pollution? You're on it! You got this big Vacuum Dirigible. The pilot's an Americorps Volunteer. She's a deaf Afro-American handicapped lesbian. It sort of floats around, you know, the blimp, wherever, and sucks up all the PARTICULATE matter. *Whisshlppp!* When it's full they come down and empty it onto this solar-powered conveyor belt, it runs into this recycled bulk milk tank, and they add hemp fiber from Canada—'cause we're not allowed to grow it here yet—and alcohol made from dairy goat whey, and they make it into electric lawnmower housings and shit—

Hey talking about lawnmowers, did you hear about the new SUSTAINABLE golf course over by Lake Champlain? It's still only nine holes, but the grass is totally non-GMO. They got runoff buffers, native plants everywhere, pre-White Man's Conquest, and they use recycled water from senior assisted living homes. Grayest fuckin' water in the state. Hey, you wanna come play with me tomorrow? I think I may skip class. I'm not feelin' it.

Oh. No problem. That's fine.

Really. Say hi to her for me.

. . . . .

2

Why am I where?

You mean, here at the workshop?

Believe me, like I haven't been looking around and asking myself the same thing.

I told you: professional development.

What?

Well, actually, no, okay, it's not professional development. Cause my company doesn't really know I'm here—I'm on my own nickel, too. So, it's more like Continuing Ed.

It's just, I needed to think about all this stuff, like from a different angle, and I saw the ad on one of the websites I track. "Learn to Write About Nature and the Environment." So I thought I'd come up and—

NO, it is not. They'll let anybody come here.

I am not SPYING. And anyway, I PAID for it. I'm a PARTICIPANT. I really am. I'm branching out.

What I do? I told you two minutes ago!

It's not that bad. It's kind of a grassroots thing. You know, hearts and minds? You listen to people, find out what their concerns are, see if you can help out. Contribute. You try to make people comfortable with stuff they might not totally agree with if they really thought about it—it's like those little pills you take when you go on a trip and think you might vomit.

Yeah.

No. I sleep fine.

Well, if I didn't do it, someone else would. So it might as well be me makin' the money. It's a job. I mean, you don't have to totally believe in a job to do it, right?

What?

No, you're right. I'm just talking about myself here, not asking YOU to—

Do I have to spell it out? The economy is still tanked! It's a buyer's market, you know what that means? It means there's eighty people lining up for every job, so unless you want an unpaid internship somewhere, maybe you have to put your principles in a drawer and go make some money, that's capitalism, sometimes you just have to hold your nose and do what you can to pay the rent and feed your wife and kids—

No I don't, I mean not right now, but someday I might—

Seriously. Eventually. Have a son, teach him about fishing and stuff.

You're not? Why not?

The planet? What's wrong with the planet?

Oh come on, that's only a theory—you don't really—

Yeah, well, there's tons of scientists that DON'T agree with it, but try to read about them in the liberal press.

Could we talk about something else?

Good.

. . .

Who, me?

Follow you? No, I didn't. I mean, well, yeah, I SAW you. But, I came right up to you. From the front. So like, how is that following?

Well.

I saw you yesterday, too. I noticed you. I was thinking, there's a good look—the work gloves, the tattoo, the dreads, dirty knees. I mean, your momma's probably not showing off any recent pictures of you at her club, but hey.

I'll bet you clean up nice.

You're welcome.

I think you should lose the shorts though.

That's NOT what I meant. I mean, go and swap them for some others.

Because. Where'd you get 'em?

I thought so. I saw the logo. Did you know that's a survivalist catalogue? So when you buy stuff from it, did you know you're supporting Stone-Age Right Wing Gonzos in Idaho with razor wire and pit bulls and AK-47's and four wives in prairie dresses, all got the same hairdo? Bet ya didn't know that.

Yeah, you see—

Well I have to. You should, too. Whoever you are, you got to read the enemy's publicity.

All right, well, for example, you're probably a pacifist, right, well, looking at you, I'm not sure of that, but, you're against perpetual war, anyway, am I right?

Yeah, so, you oughta have the new U.S. Army Physical Readiness Manual in that back pocket of yours, did you hear about it? Just been redone. There's always something you can learn, you can use it against them—you know, the latest in man to man, I mean man to woman combat, enhanced interrogation, psycho tactics—

What?

I don't know. Probably sell it in that catalogue you got the tough shorts from— Page 32, right next to the nerve gas and the powdered anthrax helper.

. . .

So, where you from?

Wow. you're far from home. How do you get back for Christmas and all?

Yeah. You see, I knew that.

No. I won't tell. Sometimes you have to.

Oh: have you heard about carbon upsets? The donation shit you can buy when you get your plane ticket. So you don't feel so guilty polluting the upper tropo.

Yeah.

No. Not OFFsets. They're lame. Carbon UPsets. That's when you feel really REALLY ashamed about what you're doing. So, you wanna do something more than just send ten bucks to a sustainable glacier-meltwater catfish farm in Chile. Carbon UPsets. You can send money to, like, illegal things? Monkey wrench gangs, graffiti artists, people who blow up train tracks and shit. I mean those people need money too. You know, to buy laptops, respirators, spray paint, trip wire, blasting caps—

Where do you get what?

Upsets? I don't know. I've never DONE it. I think you have to go to where you can buy the other stuff, and then request it. It's like those locked aisles in the video store where you gotta ask the guy with the pimples to buzz you in. The triple X's.

No. Course not. I just know they're there. Never actually—

Thanks. Well, you see? You can't always tell. Just 'cause I look like the kind of asshole that—

. . .

Hey, what's that you just pulled up?

A what?

A WILD leek? What for?

Oh. Are they any good?

Yeah. Okay. Could you like rinse it off first? You got a water bottle?

Thanks.

Tell who?

Oh. About the place. No, I'm not gonna tell. Seriously, like, go back to Kenmore and holler HEY you all wanna know where the best freakin' wild leek FORAGING grounds in northern Vermont are? Not gonna happen.

Don't ya have to cook 'em, or—

Oh.

What? Come on, like, EVERYTHING? Totally raw? What about coffee and shit?

Spring water, huh? What, you go out in the woods and DOWSE for it and dig a hole? Suck it up through a cattail stalk—

. . .

Hmm, yeah it's pretty good. Make your breath smell, though.

Thanks. I wasn't even gonna try.

So, I guess we won't starve out here.

Well, YOU don't look like you're starving. Got some fatty tissue in the right places—

Just kidding. What, can't take a sexist joke? Hey, you wanna go get a beer?

No, there's a roadhouse down by the blinking

light. Went there two nights ago. They got one of those old jukeboxes still plays vinyl.

Cool.

Nice.

. . .

So what is this, I'm gonna get the Raw Food Diet Beer Exception? They COOK the barley you know. To make the brew. I mean it's sprouted first, so maybe that qualifies.

I got it. Like, MOST of the time.

I agree. It's important to be flexible. I won't tell your buddies.

Yeah.

That's fine. You can buy your own. That way, there's no obligation.

3

Yeah, sure I'll wait. Don't change them just 'cause I said so.

Fine.

Yeah you'll want your work pants. They do a serious leg check down there. Plus, it might get cold later.

Yeah, we could. Maybe. I always go bushwhacking in the pitch dark. Sure.

So, so, what is that, your apartment up there?

Residence hall. Got it. So, you're still a STUDENT. Figured you for older.

Oh. You're kidding me, right? They let someone like YOU do that?

Huh. You teach, too?

You got some kind of ADVANCED degree?

No way. You just don't look like you're—

Right. I shouldn't. Still, I'm not gonna lie: I drive up here with my kid on the first day of school, and we're lugging in the trunks and the pennants and fridge and the TV and—

WHAT? No TV? Are you crazy?

Whatever. And YOU come out with your STUDENT LIFE COUNSELOR badge on, I take one look at YOU and I'm like, "Son, put those back in the car, we're gonna go back home and re-think this college thing, maybe go for a gap year—"

Just kiddin' you.

No, thanks. I'll wait. Nice porch. Lookit all those mountain bikes.

. . .

. . .

So, uh, thanks for coming along. I mean it. You're the first person said squat to me outside of class.

I don't know. Why did you?

Thanks. Huh. I don't really think of myself that way.

Look in the mirror? Not much. Funny. Do YOU? Don't answer. I know you do. You have to. The look you got, it takes a lot of work.

Like, attention to detail. I mean, you got that nice off the shoulder thing going with the T-shirt. Show your tan off.

Oh. Yeah. Right, your work stretches it out. In the neckline. Tell me another one. You're getting more interesting all the time.

And tell me you didn't just rip it a little down there so we'd all see the tattoo.

Yeah, you see? I could tell. Least you're honest, I'll give ya that. That kind of casual takes a lot of work. Hey let me see it again. Turn around.

Nice. But, you don't think, ten years from now, your daughter's gonna say mommy why do you have that chainsaw tattoo right over your butt crack?

Right, you're not planning to. You said so. But things happen.

I mean, like certain NORMAL PHYSICAL ACTIVITIES take place, and then things happen.

Not happening, eh?

You never know, you could be one of those metro types takes each individual case on its merit, and not just because of the specific gender—

I know what you SAID, but what you look like, I was thinking you might not be, you know, oriented—maybe you weren't born that way, could be more like a lifestyle choice thing—

Absolutely. None of my business.

You're right. I'll shut right up. Always hope, though.

. . .

So, what kinda chainsaw is it? I mean, is it a product placement?

I mean, does the company pay you for the skin space, or, are you the real thing?

You know, a tree cutter.

Me?

No, course not. Can't you tell?

I'm not gonna PRETEND I'm something I'm not, you know what I mean? Specially around you.

I've hiked around with some loggers though. Once or twice. Checkin' out transmission line corridors, you know—Hold on. Let me see your hands.

Wow. Can't hide that. Gets under the fingernails.

So, can I take a closer look?

At the tattoo.

Yeah. Wow. I like the red chain brake. Tip guard. Nice. Good safety feature. Is that a four-teen-inch bar?

Sixteen. Sweet. Shoulda known that.

Nice bumper spikes. I'm liking how the fuel filler cap kind of incorporates your mole.

So, what kind of vibration reduction system do you have? See if it's one I'm used to—

No, just kidding, I don't know shit. Only what I read. I'll bet you got sawdust in your back pockets, too.

No I don't want to check.

What, I can check? Okay, here goes, you asked—

. . !

Wow. Damn! Where'd you learn that? Ouch. Man, you coulda warned me.

No, fine, fine. Soon as I get some ice on it. What do you call that move?

Yeah. The Brazilian thing. I've seen it on TV. Don't you need a big stick or something?

I got that. You don't have a stick, you can just use your foot. Damn! So, the boots have a steel toe?

Titanium, huh.

Whoa. Thanks.

No, the ground's pretty soft.

It's okay. I'll have 'em dry-cleaned. Man, they teach that stuff here?

Oh, YOU do. Shoulda guessed. I better sign up for the class.

Oh. Well, I'll be the first guy. Men have to know self-defense, too. Look at me, I almost just lost my kneecap.

No, I'll walk it off.

Accepted. No prob. You need the chance to practice. Next time, aim a little lower, okay?

You going my way?

Thanks. Where were we before—?

Right, sawdust in your pocket.

Yeah. The chainsaw. You really good at it and all, or, just learning? They give you a free tramp stamp when you hit immortality level or something?

Oh.

Oh. Wow. What else do you teach?

Wilderness First Response. Great. Look what you did to me. What ever became of "First Do No Harm?"

Management. Hey, I did that, we—

Oh. Woodlands.

Sustainable. Now see that's what I don't understand. I mean, what's sustainable about going into a little piece of woods, and you're only gonna take like six mixed hardwood trees an acre so you have to choose just the right one, right?

Yeah.

So, you pick six, and then they get all hung up on the other trees you had to leave standing, or you gotta drag your logs out zig zag, 'cause you don't have a permit to build a road, you rip up all the underbrush, wreck the stream bed, and you get stuck, your diesel fuel leaks out, you kill six cute little muskrat babies, then you finally make it down to the road, the big smoking diesel comes along, hauls your logs to a veneer guy, and HE makes paneling for the board room of some Fortune 500 company makin' billions off female slave labor in China—how SUSTAINABLE is that? You're still in bed with the enemy—

No I am NOT, and we're not in bed—

Right.

I got it. But, is that really better than a nice neat clear cut, you cart away all the trash wood, take it to the boiler, heat your downtown with it, replant with a reliable GMO pulpwood you make money on it right back in twenty years? Or, now you've got a nice mountain cleared off, you can put wind turbines on it. Green energy, yeah. Flatten it out.

Stick ten Washington Monuments up there, hang rotors on them, you can power all the little electric cars in the whole state.

No, I'm saying I might agree with you more if you thought it through like I did.

Right, maybe you have.

You're right, I'm not letting you. So how would I know? Sorry.

So, what DO you think?

Wow.

I never—

Isn't wind power a good thing? Anyway, I thought it was a done deal, I—

Hey, I'm sorry, I didn't mean to—

Wow. Fine. Talk about it later.

. . .

Here's my car. They make you park back behind all the buildings, so everyone can pretend nobody drove to get here.

It's a Buick.

No, my grandma didn't die. I bought it.

Why not? It's a pride thing. It's American-made. Or most of it is anyway.

No you probably haven't. That's 'cause everyone up here drives foo-foo hybrids, or rusty old pickups. But like, this is the best-selling new car in China.

No shit.

The Chinese, they're eating hamburgers, smokin' Marlboros, drinkin' real Burgundy, buying

Picassos, building fake stucco gated communities, tuckin' their eyelids, and driving Buicks, why do you think GM got out of bankruptcy so soon? You think it's 'cause your man Obama bailed them out? I don't think so. Hell, they'd even buy Oldsmobiles if we still made 'em.

Wait I gotta throw this stuff in the back. Wasn't expecting company.

What?

Sure.

Really. It's fine. You can drive. Here.

Nice catch. It's the big silver one.

No, I'm okay with it. Women can drive, run a chainsaw, pee standing up, kick me in the shin, or, you know, forget all about me and screw each other silly or whatever you guys do, I never could figure that out. . . . It's cool. Whatever you want.

Make a left, yeah.

What?

The transmission? Yeah, it is, it's a bit sloppy.

Yeah, I noticed it. Only when you're goin' down a hill, though.

No, you don't have to.

I'm sure you could. But you'd get your back all dirty.

It's okay, I'll take it in when I get home. It's still on warranty.

. . .

It's out past the general store. Couple three miles. You never went?

Oh. Right. I forgot. I can't believe they really got one of those around here. Is it like, for all kinds, I mean, BLT's or whatever?

Right. Sorry. LGBT.

And Q. So where is it, up by Canada, get *zose femme Franch gurrls* to come *ovair zee bordair*? *Zoot alor, mah new gurrrl-fran she eez ze one wiz ze eh saw chain, down zere.*

Nice.

No, I never been to one. Never got invited I guess.

. . .

Feels good with the windows down, don't it? Good clean air up around here. Gonna be a nice night.

Never sat over here before.

It's fine. Man, look at that swamp. It's huge! We don't see a moose tonight, I'm saying they're just a fairy tale.

Seriously? Where?

Wow. Well, I'm lookin'. Hope they come out tonight.

Really? When?

Wow. How big was it?

No shit. I can't believe that! So, I guess you just walked up to it and beat it dead with your cappucino stick.

Capoeira. Right.

No way!

How many shots did you—?

Damn. You cut it up and everything?

MOOSE KILLER! Kiss ka say—better run run run run run run RUN AWAYYYYYYY!

What's it taste like?

Well that's a big help, I never ate one of those either.

But I mean, how many pounds did it weigh?

What, just the meat? Damn, what'd you do with it all?

Wow, that's a shitload of burgers. Where is it now?

Where, in the walk-in? Wait, you don't feed it to the students, do ya?

But, isn't there some kind of STATE LAW? What if they all get chronic MAD MOOSE disease or something? Guys get antler-on-the-brain. I knew it! You are all TOTALLY CRAZY up here.

I mean, you wonder why college is so expensive. The liability insurance must be—

Yeah, yeah, I know. "Release from Harm." I've seen 'em. "My son slash daughter has my permission to attend Black Fly Tech. My son slash daughter has my permission to eat mooseburgers, raw milk, compost grubs, vegan fake cheese cake. I understand that attending college involves ENORMOUS risk to my son slash daughter, including but not limited to deer tick bites, poison ivy, heartworm, rock slides, flash floods, indoctrination into fanatic lesbian sex cults by tattooed combat-ready dormitory counselors—"

. . .

So, what do you drive?

Ha. You can field-strip a GM tranny but you don't like OWN A CAR?

You got a license, though; right?

Oh.

No, that's fine. Not a problem.

Yeah, really.

. . . . .

4

This is it.

Cool. You're welcome.

Man, if I collected anything, it'd be neon signs. I really like how they glow. And, you know, there's nothing bad you environmentalists can say about inert gasses.

Oh yeah? No, I didn't know that.

Or that either. You probably worked in an argon mine or something, before you became a kick boxer watershed analyst.

Hey before we go in, could you take a little look at this thing on my ankle? I think it's alive. It jumped me when we were back there talkin'. I guess I stood still too long.

Yeah.

Ouch.

Damn. It's not one of those Lyme disease thingees, is it? Sucking my—

Right, way too big. Wow, nice knife! Where'd that come from all of a sudden?

Cool. You want me to stick it between my teeth or something?

Okay.

. . .

Thanks. Oo. So, that's the best way, you think? Take the whole thing and a pound of calf muscle too—

I did say thank you. There's some kleenex in the back seat, yeah.

. . .

It's kind of nice just to sit here, isn't it? I like it when the engine shuts off, sun's goin' down, blinkin' neon, Rasta girl beside you in the driver's seat—

I guess I'm a poet.

Hey could we not go in for a minute. could we play like TRUTH OR DARE or something? I want to tell you something. Okay?

Thanks.

Okay. Here goes: I'm not, I'm not really up here for professional development, no, or continuing ed, or industrial spying either like you said.

Sorry. You want to know the truth? It's weird, I kinda feel I have to tell you the truth. Whole truth and nothing but.

Okay. I don't work for a power company. I mean, it's almost true, or it WAS, 'cause I worked for a company that like, SOLD power companies. Bought and sold. Did you know you can flip utilities like you can flip houses? Bet you didn't know that.

Good, I know there had to be something you didn't know—

No, I wasn't really lying, I mean the job was really what I said, I was like a facilitator, a lubricator—

You know what I mean. But, the truth is I was terminated.

Fired. Yeah. You can call it that.

No, not actually just. It was five months ago. Which is actually why my wife split. Athough I was about to leave her.

Yeah. we had like a race to see who would leave who first—did you ever do that?

Oh so you know what I mean.

Yeah, you're right, that can be harder for a girl, I mean a woman—

Right, or if the guy is real possessive or violent or something.

You're right. Totally.

No I'm not. I swear. I mean, HER temper was way worse than mine.

I guess she suddenly saw she was hitching herself to the wrong wagon, you know what I mean?

Why'd they do what?

Fire me? Oh, 'cause they could see my heart wasn't in it anymore. they got people workin' for them their only job is sniffing workers like me out. Turns out I was the one about to vomit.

Yeah.

Man it's like, I can talk to you.

I mean, you just look at me like that, and it's like I took truth serum or something.

With who?

No, she never wanted to talk about anything. With me. I mean, nothing real. Just, you know, shopping and stuff. Her mom was the same way, I couldn't believe the stuff they talked about. She called her every day.

. . .

Okay.

That was it.

I mean, that was mine. You gonna do it too?

. . .

Wow.

See, I knew it. I had a feeling. Not that I would have tried to convince you or anything.

Totally. I understand.

So what made you go over? Other than, obviously, being one tough bitch yourself.

Sorry. Tough woman.

You're right. I'll shut up.

Oh man no! How did you let that happen?

Shit.

Ouch.

Ow. Let's see.

No they did a good job. Really. They look fine. I couldn't tell. They give you any trouble eatin' corn on the cob or—

Good. What a bastard. I hope you had him arrested.

Wow.

You did the right thing. He was never gonna change. People who do that kind of shit, you know, beat up women, ruin your life, ruin everyone's life, they're never EVER gonna change.

Yeah.

I'll bet he gave you warnings, right?

Yeah. Tons of them. I mean, you probably weren't even surprised when it happened. That's the thing I—

I know. But still, it's hard to see how a smart woman—

I guess so.

You beat him up though, right? I mean look at the move you did on me—

Oh, that's why.

Well now at least you know how, if it ever happens again.

No, that's right. Never gonna happen again.

So, that sort of sent you in the other direction, right?

I can see that.

Yeah, you get afraid to jump back in. You'd actually have to deal with your opposite again. Not that anything is really opposite anymore.

I mean you know, everything is circular now. Gender. You can jump on anywhere. It's all good. Like a big ferris wheel—whatever car you get on, eventually you're up at the top, and swinging, and the view—

Hey why are you looking at me like that?

Thanks.

No, I've really thought about it. I read stuff, too. I read a lot.

I'm surprising you, right?

Cool.

What?

I came that close, huh?

Well, I'm glad you didn't.

Thanks. Ya see? Just goes to show.

. . .

So, what about that beer? I'm a little dry.

. . . . .

5

So, tell me if I'm wrong, I get this feeling we're not going in yet, right?

Well, we're still sitting here, for one thing.

What?

What smell? MY smell?

Oh that. That's my aftershave. I put too much on?

What, you don't like the scent?

Well, that doesn't surprise me. First off, probably nobody up here even OWNS a razor.

You're all into hair. Like you, you got hair in places, I'm not gonna lie, you would have been laughed off the schoolbus.

I figured that. Is it like some kind of cult thing with you? Like, Jah Rule or something? Legalize eet?

That's a relief. But the guys, they must think

they can get more chicks if they're fuzzy. "We're all vegan, so we don't even kill the hairs on our own cheeks."

Oh right. The mooseburgers. You're right. They couldn't be.

Yeah, matter of fact, I do. Every day.

I don't know. Habit, I guess. From when I was working.

No. I went back to the dorm after dinner and put more on, 'cause of goin' for a walk outside. I figured it'd keep the pumas away. They don't like Old Spice Classic.

Catamounts. Whatever.

Okay. Catamounts. Absolutely.

Yeah, I read about that. It was on a dairy farm near here, right?

I knew that. That's why I thought—

Yeah. Didn't they take an impression of the paw print, and like send the shit, I mean, what's it called?

Right. The scat, didn't it get taken to the State Scat Lab to be analyzed?

Yeah, nobody ever saw it again. I heard about that. I mean, who's gonna ACCIDENTALLY lose a quart bag of stinking steaming catamount caca?

"So, uh, thank you very much Farmer Jones, excellent work, we'll just take that off your hands, send it up for analysis, appreciate you drivin' all the way up here, how are the crops doing, here's my card, call me if it comes back—"

Seriously, if they ever CONFIRM a native mountain lion sighting up here, the whole forestry business in Vermont'll get locked up. Biggest endangered species shutdown in history. Never gonna happen. They could find ten happy mountain lion families living up here in the woods, and they'll all be like, yeah, must have escaped from some exotic farm, some rich guy's petting zoo like that creep in Indiana—just, keep on cuttin' those trees down, don't ever turn off the chainsaw though, and, keep looking around, don't work alone, bring a friend, bring a camera—

Why? I don't know.

I wish I knew. It's how my mind works. I just, I KNOW about shit like this. It's weird.

Once I see something, or hear something, by accident, it's like my mind is stuck with it forever, even if I'll never ever use it. I'll pick up a magazine in some doctor's office, and then I'm like, look at this article. This farmer up in Vermont sees a mountain lion outside his kitchen window. Now, someday, you never know, you may be up there, you might meet this WOODS WOMAN, and you're gonna go have a beer with her, you want to be able to talk about this shit, so read on—

Yeah. It just does it automatically. With all the details. My mind: it's that vacuum blimp sucking up all the garbage in the air.

Oh yeah? Well maybe we're kindred spirits then.

So, what do YOU use?

Please stay with us. We are now returning to a previous place in the conversation. I mean, what product.

No, we've established that you don't shave. Or wax. Or tweeze. Anywhere. I mean, like for your skin. Or what about the hair? Don't you ever need to get the dreadlocks unstuck, or—

Forget it. You probably don't need anything. I mean, look at you—

What do I mean? I mean you're so CLEAN!

You know. Clean!

Did you ever read THE LEOPARD? It's this Italian novel. These two old guys are sitting at a café in Sicily, out on the street, drinkin' grappa, and Monica Bellucci or whoever walks by in this skin tight skirt, walkin' so slow you can hear her two thighs rubbing against each other like, I don't know, like two eggplants sizzling in Extra Extra Virgin olive oil, and one of the two dudes turns to the other and says "her sheets must smell like paradise."

I thought about that when I saw you, no kidding. Sorry if that's, like, not appropriate, but—

—You're welcome—

—let me finish. It's different. I mean, you're natural, not like squeaky clean or anything. Americans don't like to smell real stuff anymore anyway, they gotta have everything sanitized, they go to some island paradise they read about, in the

Bahamas, and they want AC, air fresheners, hand-cleaner dispensers, they want it all to look and smell like a Hampton Inn—

Who?

Oh, her. Yeah, totally, she was EXACTLY like that! I don't know how we ever—

Yeah, I know. I said it before.

So then I go out for a walk and I start thinking about this assignment I have to write, and all of a sudden YOU jump out from behind that tree, like you were waiting to pounce—

You were too.

Were too!

Okay, sorry! And then, you move in real close, and my nostrils click in and I get this whiff of cedar and mushrooms and apple cider, and spearmint, it's impossible for my brain to process, let alone forget, plus add what you freaking LOOK like, with the dreads and the henna and the ripped shirt and the ink and the tongue stud, the mountain boots—I got it all right away, trust me.

What?

Where what?

Right. Back to that. We now take you to ANOTHER previous part of the conversation.

Sorry. Well it wasn't in the campus bookstore. You don't even have one here. I bought it at the Rite-Aid back by the interstate. Stopped to update my toilet kit. I actually read somewhere it keeps WILD ANIMALS away, but obviously it doesn't work 'cause look, here YOU are sitting right there, and you got my car keys in your paw too, and the big knife. I may not get outta here alive. And I didn't tell anyone where I was going.

Okay, I could do that. Never been asked before. But, for you—

You're welcome. You got some kind of chemical sensitivity or something? The gym I work out in—there's a sign says please don't use scented anything—

That's good, but still, you're saying you want me to—

All right. When?

Hmm. What's the correct answer here?

How about, "as soon as I can?"

No?

Hmm. How about, "right now?"

Whew. Good. Got that one right.

Um, I don't know; how would YOU answer that if I asked you, let's see—ah, got it, how about we go stick my head in a waterfall?

Yeah! High-five!

Ow!

I'm sure you do. We walk or drive?

Right. Fine. Little detour.

No. You're doin' fine. Start it up. Watch backin' out, that pickup just pulled in a little close.

. . .

This mean you'll dance with me?

I can live with that.

. . . . .

6

. . .

. . .

. . .

Hey I kind of liked that, actually. Clears the head right up.

Yeah. There's a couple in the trunk. I'll pop it. In the laundry box.

Nice. Do I smell better now?

Thanks.

Watch it, don't get too close.

Cause I might get you back for holding my head under so long. And the kick too.

Right. And the knife wound. That too. Thanks for reminding me.

I don't know, I'd figure something out.

I know you did. But I didn't hold you under. And you were just doing it for solidarity or whatever.

It's funny though, your hair looks EXACTLY the same wet as it does dry. No "before" and "after." It's like peat moss, no, concrete or something. High absorption factor—like those rugs you can rent for your office door. For shoes to drip on.

Oh man.

Nothing.

Did anyone ever tell you you look absolutely awesome when you smile? Your upper lip kind of flattens out—

Right. Sorry.

Yeah, let's go.

What?

Oh, thanks. You'll hafta navigate though. I didn't really watch all the turns.

You gotta admit it handles nice.

I mean, Americans used to know how to build cars. We taught the world. I don't know what happened.

You know, with everything. Our manufacturing, engineering—

They do? They teach that stuff here—well, maybe I should just move up here, take classes, and find out all that free trade shit, and get re-educated. I need something—

I don't know. It just kind of happened. My wife's dad was in the business. Took me right out of college. I think it was part of the deal.

Yeah, the marriage. So I said, fine, I'll work a few years, pay off my loans, then I'll quit and do what I really want to do, not that I knew what that was—

Yeah maybe. I never really tried it. Free-lancing—I don't know.

But then, I got in so deep I had the 90 dollar haircut and the pants and Italian shoes. Next I started trash talking like a black basketball player—

Damn right. You have to.

You're a young trader or whatever and you come to the office all scrubbed and pink, you look down at your fingers on the keyboard and you're like whoa how did I get to look like this, smell like this, so then you have to over-compensate, act like mister caveman, you start cursing, put a lot of fuckin this fuckin that in your speeches, pretty soon the testosterone starts gushing—

I swear to God! Middle managers? They talk like stevedores, or at least like stevedores used to talk back in the day—now they're all Chinese or Filipinos—

Yeah, no, you start saying fuck, and shit, and sit on a stick—

Whew! Listen to you! Yeah, all of those, too.

Whoa! And that. Which is gonna sound funny, you know, to the outside ear, 'cause it's these wusses in suits and manicures talking about bundled energy futures and utility debt default swaps but you add motherfuckin and cocksuckin in your speech and suddenly you're powerful, you start standing with your legs a few inches more apart, you act like you're this western FRONTIER dude coming in for a shoot-out in a saloon, but the thing is once you start doing that you can't stop, you have to keep it up or the next guy in line will blow you off the boardwalk. That's how it is, it's cut-throat.

You got to act tougher, which means riskier, than the guy standing next to you or you're toast, so like, eventually shit, REALLY BAD SHIT, happens, stuff that can mess up the whole world economy, but no one PERSON is responsible, and there's also no one holding anyone else back—

Yeah, and I was making buckets of money. Even after I got demoted. Got my loans paid. But man—

I don't know. I don't know where it all went.

Yeah, to her. A lot. I only saved up enough for me for a couple of months while I'm up here figuring it out. You gonna help me?

No. What I MEAN by that is, do you have it all figured out so you can TELL me. Not like oh help hold my hand and we'll go figure it out together.

. . .

Thanks. That felt nice.

Took me by surprise.

Yeah. Kind of like back in junior high school. Then you start wondering who's gonna let go first.

. . .

. . .

So, uh, what you drinking?

No, I said. You can pay for your own. Fine. You're the one still earning a paycheck.

Look, I'm just placing your ORDER, okay? Makin' conversation with Maxine. You remember me from a couple nights ago, right Max?

Oh. Well I remember you.

Two IPA's.

. . .

Over there?

Nice. A little out of the public eye. But still, near where the crowd is. Your butch buddies happen to come in and see you, they don't automatically think we're together or anything.

Cool.

That's the best attitude to have.

Well, I'm really glad you did.

Cheers. Lookin' at you.

. . .

Mmm, that's good. Worth the wait.

You don't smoke do you?

Neither do I.

Yeah it is. Cause now we'd have to go back outside, and we just got here.

. . .

I think I just ran out of stuff to say. Got distracted maybe.

It's probably 'cause you're lookin' at me funny.

Um, it's hard to say. Like you're, I don't know, makin' some kind of plan?

See I knew it. You gonna tell me?

Yeah I can.

No rush. I'm gonna go check out the juke box. You like the Dixie Chicks?

Damn right. FUCK George Bush.

If they have "Mister Heartache" will you dance with me?

Cool.

. . .

Score!

After you.

Love walked out on me
And didn't even close the door
Next thing I know I'm starin'
At your shadow on the floor. . .

So, uh, nice to see people up here still know how to slow dance.

You're right, sometimes it's the only thing that works. I mean, people make it out to be hard or something, but you just gotta get your mind out of the way. Walk around in the box. Don't kick the other person's toes.

Sure you can. I was kind of expecting that. I let you drive my car didn't I?

Gotta hold me harder though. So you can let me know where you're going. I'll just put my hand—ssssssssst! Man!

It's the tattoo. I musta touched your spark plug housing. It's overheating.

So, you weren't planning to connect, right? Swung nice and slow so I could duck?

Thanks.

. . .

This is really nice.

You gonna tell me the plan yet?

Okay. The next one's a slow dance too.

Yeah two for a quarter. Old school.

I wouldn't be a man
if I didn't feel like this
I wouldn't be a man
if a woman like you
was anything I could resist

No reason. I like the guy's voice. Deeeeep. Never actually listened to the words.

Makes sense.

All those dudes, they learned how to sing in church, and they're all like still singing right out of the hymn book. Jesus songs. They just, you know, change a word or two, they got them a pop tune. Home is the chapel, wife is the preacher, and the guy's the congregation gettin' hollered at 'cause they've been sinful, and prayin' is when the guy asks for forgiveness and she makes him get down on his knees and start—

Okay. No prob.

. . .

I like this one.

. . .

Hey, did something just happen?

I mean, you stopped leading.

Sure, just follow. Like they taught you in gym class.

Fine. Go ahead. Lean in, just put it right there.

Yeah, it's okay. Feels good. Rest my chin on ya.

Kind of like, sunbathing on a pile of bricks, but, a guy can get used to a lot of discomfort in the name of love.

Yeah women too I guess.

Yeah no it just popped into my head.

You're right. When we sit down I'll write it down on a napkin. It's just one line though, I don't know what the rest of the song's about.

I guess we will, won't we?

. . .

You didn't answer my question.

About something happening.

To me? Yeah, absolutely.

Describe it? Okay. Um, all of a sudden it was like there wasn't anyone else here. You know how in a dream, you're in a crowd, with someone, and then you look around and it's just the two of you. But 'cause it's in a dream everyone else can get wiped out in a second. Boom.

Did I say something wrong?

No, I mean, BESIDES the seventy-four other wrong things I said in the last two hours.

Like I said, my brain sucks up this stuff, and

then, the way it's programmed, if I'm talking, I usually riffle through all the possibles in a second and then come out with the WRONGEST thing to say. I think it started out as a disease, on the spectrum you know? But now it's a matter of pride. Go look at my file down at Mass General. They're gonna name the condition after me.

So yeah I probably did.

Say something wrong.

I didn't?

It happened to you too?

What I was describing, feeling like something just happened—

Oh. What was yours?

. . .

You're welcome. You want another?

No. Another beer.

Okay.

Hey, me too. I mean, the men's.

Cool. Meet you back here, and then we can head.

You're right. Way too nice.

. . . . .

7

Yeah it's much nicer out here.
Sure. Walking is good. Dancing is better, but—
Up to the light and back, maybe?

. . .

Remember what I said WHEN?
I mean, I've said lots of stuff to ya.
Yeah—
Flipping? Oh, yeah. Flipping power companies.
Yeah. I know all about that. It's what I used to do. After they moved me over to PR. Although, I gotta tell you the truth, I was just a hack. Handing out stuff to help people get comfy. Or, you know, stickin' free pens and stuff in plastic bowls at Energy Expos—
You know, trade shows. Putting on my smile. Like this.
Yeah.
You been to places like that, you know—

Okay, you haven't, but you can imagine—

Wow. All right. I'll explain it. You're in a big convention hall, right? In Denver, Baltimore... Lot of fluorescent lighting. Not a piece of real wood anywhere. There's down time. Plenty of it. You leave your goodies in your booth. You go take a piss, get some coffee, maybe step outside for a minute, get some real air. Or, what passes for air in Soot City. You go back in, walk around and see who else is showcasing, right? You see people you recognize from the last one, someone you had some Kool-Aid with last time. Take a look at what they're giving out, you pick up a lot of printed stuff, you go back, sit in your folding chair and you read it.

You with me?

Yeah, most of it's bullshit.

Don't get me wrong, there's lots of really honest people, deep thinkers, engineers, innovators actually. Inventors. Workin' on CRAZY stuff. Algae pools. Cheap geothermal. That vacuum blimp? They're working on it. Solar roof paint. Concave collectors. Heat pumps. Whirling wind generators at the end of a string—

Yeah. I'm not just making it up—.

Damn right. If they ever build it. But. For every one of those, there's two or three booths that you know are just lying, right, like if it's wind they're telling you their turbine, the only prototype they ever actually put up anywhere, has a capacity factor of 45% when you know it never hit 20, except for a couple of minutes in hurricane season just before they had to pop the clutch.

Well yeah, you know what would happen if they didn't do that—

That's right. See it running away down the hill, cartwheeling—

Just like in a fairy tale. Peasants running out of their farmyards, shriekin', tryin' to get out of the way—

Where was I. Oh yeah, then there's these booths of totally CREEPY people who don't actually have anything to sell, they just want to like sneak in and see how they can get to be the fine print you never actually read on your electric bill, like Enron was, fuckin' low life bastards never MADE a thing, just sucked people's money, bankrupted California.

Well that's true, but, for every one that DOES get caught, you know how that is, there's dozens who get away with it—

Exactly. And, while they're busy getting away with it, they got their lobbyists buying up Senators so the next time they do it it'll be totally legal.

Yeah, you could say so. Till I quit.

Okay. Right. I did say that. Thanks for reminding me. But I was ABOUT to quit.

So what do you want to know?

Yeah.

Yeah.

I told you I heard about it. Industrial wind. I haven't seen it, but—

Yeah, I saw that article, and people were talking in the dining hall today, one of your professor buddies—

She's totally right. It doesn't make sense here. No sense. I mean, in the midwest, yes. Kansas, wherever, there's thousands of them, you fly over them, they make the coolest shadows if it's the right time of day—

Right, nothing. No mountains, no valleys. Nothing. One big wind tunnel, from the Rockies to the Ozarks. That's the place for it.

So you want to know who let them—

Yeah. I'd want to know that, too. I'd say, follow the money.

Okay.

For starters, let's agree on one thing here. Okay? What I've read, it's not about getting us off foreign oil. I don't care what they say. It has NOTHING TO DO WITH THAT!

Sorry.

But you can put that to rest. And, it's not about clean energy for Vermonters, either, right?

No. Because only about ten percent of it is gonna go to Vermont. The rest is for, up to Canada. I mean it's not gonna produce all the time, but when it does, most of it's heading north. Or, lighting those office buildings all night long in the Big Apple.

I know that. Not tellin' ya anything you don't already know.

Let me finish. Here's something you may not know. You got someone who has a bright idea about a wind turbine—

Yeah. So they want to build it. They do a feasibility study. Get someone else to pay for that, of course. And then, before you can say Tom Edison, I mean, while it's still in the Planning Phase, a multi-national swoops in and buys the power company, right, and then do you know what they do?

They rake in all the federal subsidies, thank you very much, and the PR, the Vermont Brand, and they get the do-gooders too, the Quakers and the hippies, everyone saying Yay wow big wind towers, they're so renewable, save the planet, fight climate change, and everything that anybody writes about it adds value too, on paper, and the things get built and before the reaction sets in, like oh shit they flattened our mountaintop oh damn we thought the electricity was gonna cost a lot less, oh hell those things are butt-ugly, oh fuck we can't sleep with the thump thump thump, my kid is having seizures, oh my look at those poor dead birds, oh Jesus these things are gonna be obsolete in ten years—before all that? Before all that, the company flips it, 'cause there's always another sucker out there who wants to buy a power company.

I know. You got lucky, you hit the one thing I know about—

Do you think so?

So. Now you know everything I know. I'm just—

Excited. More than about the windmills.

Yeah.

You are?

Well, so, it's your one thing too. We ARE Kindred Spirits.

Anne of Green Gables. My favorite movie.

. . .

Sure. The night's young. Where we going?

No shit. All the way up there? Isn't it private property now?

Okay. I'm game.

Sure you don't wanna go back in and have one more dance first?

Okay.

No. I was getting used to the music. It was definitely helping. But, we can pop in a CD or something. Dance in the headlights. Where do people park around here?

Oh.

No, I was kidding.

We are? You sure you know the way?

Yeah. I actually do. They're in the car. Still in the box. Mine are REAL leather. Wait I'll put 'em on now, in the light—

That neon light—

Yeah, makes everything look special, you know what I mean?

. . .

They feel good. I may never wear loafers again.

. . .

So, which way?
Okay.

. . .

Damn.

No. I just, get the feeling it's gonna be a LONG NIGHT. I shoulda had me some nachos or something back there. Now I'm hungry. Being with you MAKES ME SO HUNGRY—

Just kidding. You don't by any chance—

Oh. Cool.

What is it?

Moose jerky? Shoulda known. Hey but back there you said you don't—

Oh. Right. No beef. You said. But moose is okay?

Makes sense. If you kill it yourself, even better.

Sure, it's a lifestyle thing.

I respect that. I really do. Course, there's 300 million Americans, and if everyone did that, there'd be blood all over the map. And flies. And friends of Dick Cheney in every E.R. with birdshot up their nose. But hey at least there wouldn't be millions of sicko FEEDLOTS heating up the planet with pure methane—so, lookin' at it that way—

Well, that's true too. We could all cut back.

We are. Way too fat. Fattest people in history. Paleo's way better. Hunter-gatherers are always gonna be mostly skinny. And have muscles, and dreadlocks, killer abs, chainsaw tattoos, and just enough fatty tissue like you do, to keep guys—

Mnnnhh—

Nnngg—

Mmnm. If you're gonna stuff it IN like that, make the pieces smaller, okay? You coulda killed me. Plus, I'm driving.

Accepted.

Actually it's good. Real good. I'll bet a little goes a long way.

Could we, like, stop at that waterfall along the way? Have another head dunk?

Oh we're not?

Where?

Really?

You'd do that? We only just—

Now you're talkin'. Wow.

Totally. I promise. WORD OF GOD.

Among friends, yeah.

. . . . .

8

Which way?

Okay.

Cool. Get to know all the back roads. Course, every fuckin' road up here is a back road.

. . .

You do?

Sure. Feel free.

Go ahead. You got me. I'm listening.

No kidding. I didn't—

Yeah—

Uh-huh.

Wait, let me get this straight. Back up there, in the woods, when I said hello, you like already KNEW who I was, you—

So, it wasn't just, an accidental meeting—

In MY way. You put yourself IN MY WAY.

Great. Some chance meeting, huh?

My essay? What essay?

I know. Everybody has to write one. I don't know, isn't it for the teachers, so they know who they're gonna have showin' up in class? But—

All of them? What, you all sit around the faculty lounge—

All right, screened-in-porch, it's BLACK FLY U. after all. What, you drink a brewski, a local micro one, eat broccoli and dip, read the applications and talk about all the wannabes who signed up for your Summer Eco-Enrichment Program—

I don't know what to say. I don't even remember what I wrote. Plus I didn't come here to study riverbank poetry with you, I came to do like journalism and—

I get it. So you're all responsible. All for one, one for all.

So, what, you read that shit whatever it was I wrote, and my resumé, and you said, "Sweet, I hafta meet this guy—"

Damn. You told me it was 'cause I was good looking. That's not fair!

Thanks. Only now I'm not so sure I trust you when you say that.

I appreciate it. But I bet you say that to all the guys whose brains you wanna pick. "Yeah pretty decent outside, let's see what's in there—"

No I'm sorry, it's just kind of a shock, that's all.

And what about back there when we were dancing? "I wouldn't be a man, if a woman like you—" And, and, you leanin' your furry head on my chest—

Well, yeah, it FELT sincere. But—

Good.

Yeah. Felt that way to me.

. . .

You mind if I pull over for a minute?

Because.

Thanks.

. . .

Damn. It is SO quiet up here, when you turn the car off.

. . .

I'm thinking. Gonna go stand outside a minute, okay?

Sure, suit yourself.

. . .

I'm about to. Hold on a minute.

. . .

Okay. I'm on your turf here. Right? I'm like WAY out of my element.

Yeah.

I mean, you could walk in, LOSE yourself anywhere up here, and survive, know what I'm saying? I saw the knife you pack, you could have conquered a whole Pacific Island with that in World War 2.

So, you're calling the shots. Am I right?

That's fine. Just, tell me where we're going, okay?

So, that's first. That's still happening, right? It's like, nearby, or, on the way—

Yeah, right, just a quick dip. Cool off. Although, to tell you the truth, it's probably not gonna cool me off.

Uh-huh. Nothing we can do about that. I mean, there IS, but—

Fine. And then what?

All right. I got the picture now. That's all I needed. The drive, the skinny dip, dot dot dot—

Okay, no dot dot dot.

ANOTHER drive, and then we park the Buick, right, as far up as we can go—find the sign—

Right. We picnic. A little moose jerky, somethin' to drink—

Spring water? Hey what about beaver fever?

Cool. Does that stuff really work?

Nice. Pop. Fizz. Swig. And then—

Yep, tuck my pants in my socks, then we go break in my new hikers.

Got it. Sometimes, I just need to know.

Yeah, that's all. It's fine. It's, it's a comfort thing. Seriously—you're three hundred miles from home, it's night time, there's no moon yet but it's coming, you're with someone you never met before tonight, a woman, I mean she's attractive, in a werewolfy way, don't get me wrong, but you know, it turns out she actually STALKED you, after the required Background Check. She's tellin' you stuff, a bit at a time, but clearly there's stuff she's not really tellin'

you, plus she has a history of violence—WITH
YOU, and you're remembering crazy scary bed-
time stories, bonfire stuff you used to hear at Cub
Scout Camp, and—

Mmmm.

Sweet. I—

Mmmm. Mmmmmm. Mmmmmmmm.

. . .

. . .

. . .

Well.

That does put a different spin on it.

I guess—

Yeah, I did. Wild leeks and all.

No, you answered them.

Really.

Fine, just tell me where I should turn.

. . .

So, I guess anytime you want to shut me up,
now you know how to do it.

. . . . .

9

Oh, man.

Wish I'd brought my Springsteen mix with me.
Like—

I remember us riding in my Buick car
her body tan and wet down at the reservoir—
Man.

YIPPPPEEEEEEEEEEEEEE!

No. Sorry. Just had to let off a little—

So, what music do you like? I mean, you're probably pretty particular.

Never heard of her. She from around here?

Thought so. What she sing about?

Oh yeah? Sing me a few lines.

Wow. She write that?

Have you, like, contacted her? She could to do a benefit. You go up against power companies, you need money—

Great. No. I didn't hear about it.

You have a nice voice. Kinda husky.

. . .

So, uh, what was it about my dossier that ATTRACTED you to me, was it—

Right. You didn't say you were. Not the word you used. Still—

Yeah. Gotta be clear on that. But, you didn't, like, run the other way—

I WAS NOT STANDING ON YOUR SHOELACE!

So, not my ex-job, right?

My writing voice? Cool. No one ever noticed that before.

So, it just sounds like a perfect storm, you know, the writing, the mind, the power company connection, the Ethan Hawke lookalike, the willingness to take abuse—

Right, no photo, you hadn't laid eyes on me yet—

You coulda been stuck with some slob, or pervert—

Right. I still could be. But, worth taking the chance. All else being equal.

Okay.

I'm opening up the letter now. I mean, I'm still driving, but I can see the glow-in-the-dark message: ahem, "Your mission, if you choose to accept it, is to stop mountaintop removal on a pristine ridgeline in the far distant Northeast

Kingdom of Vermont, sabotage the access road, halt the construction of new transmission lines heading north *oui oui for ze tres tres riche powair consumairs of Kay-beck City*, monkey wrench twenty-one five-hundred-foot turbine towers—all while RESISTING the potentially fatal attractions of Special Agent . . . "—wait, what's your name?

Oh.

Pretty. It fits. That's a fake name, right?

Of course. You'd have to.

No "e" where? Is it supposed to have an "e?"

Oh. Right.

What?

Whoa. A little advance warning next time—

That's okay. Is this really a road, or what?

I don't think my muffler's gonna clear that hump in the middle. Can we walk in?

Fine.

. . .

I left the keys in. Figure cougars don't have opposable thumbs.

Catamounts. That's what I meant.

Damn. It is frigging dark.

I'm sorry. The evening is EXTREMELY OBSCURE, perhaps the lady has noticed?

Yeah. I've heard that before. So do we just wait until our eyes adjust, that could take ten minutes, and I am NOT gonna stand here like a sitting duck till—

Okay. Which way's the—?

Okay. Yep, one foot after the other. Just keep talking so I can hear ya.

. . .

Yep, or breathe hard. That works. I can hear that. As long as it's still you.

Is it far?

Oh, nice. Don't we need to bring anything?

Good. Keep the hands free. Although, I really wouldn't mind, one hand—

Thanks. Don't let go, okay?

. . .

This is the darkest place I've ever been in. I mean, I can't even see my—Oh, wait—I can HEAR it! Hey, I think we're already there.

What, a spillway, like in a huge dam? Kind of off to the right, right?

Am I gonna get swept away?

No. By the WATER!

Good.

So we just—

Great. Fine. I like to fold mine, so—

I hope I can find them again. Well, actually who the hell cares?

. . .

Hey where are you?

Oh. Wow. That was quick. How is it?

Cool.

Don't worry, I won't. Not a real good diver anyway.

. . .

I guess you forgot to mention it's ICE COLD.
Helloooo!

. . .

Where—
Marco.
Marco?
Marco!
MARCO!
Ah.

. . .

Yeah. I can back float.
Like this?
Just like my Aunt Peggy did. When she taught
me how.
No! To swim!
Hey, watch those hands.

. . .

Wow. Look at all those stars.
That's the Dipper, huh? So the north star is—
I see it. It's hard 'cause it's not as bright as a lot
of them.
Wow.
Wow.
I AM relaxed!
Can't help that. That's got a mind of its own.

. . .

So you must know celestial navigation, right—
we'll make it back to our clothes?

Good then. Not gonna give it another thought.
. . .
Your turn.
To float.
. . .
. . !
. . . . .

10

You know, I wouldn't have believed it. It's totally true.

Seeing in the dark.

Yeah. I could actually see the STARLIGHT on the headlight lens. I mean, that's good, because the next second I was gonna smash into it with my knee.

No, the other one.

Yeah, one less injury. First injury prevented all night long. Mark that down.

If you and me are gonna hang out for any length of time, I'll just, get used to having bruises. And water in my lungs.

Oh, absolutely yes. Worth every minute.

No thanks. Not thirsty. You forgetting I took in half the pond back there? Up my nose? I won't need a drink till next Monday.

Absolutely. Logical consequences. Don't blame you at all.

Wow.

I'm just gonna sit here, never shut the door.

Cause the dome light's on, so now I can see you. I haven't seen you in a long time.

Well it FEELS like about two hours.

Until the battery's dead, I guess. Or I am, whichever comes first.

No, it's just—Sorry. It's just, you can miss something in your life and not know it, you know what I mean?

. . .

You know what they say about silence.

Yeah.

Your turn. But I'm not gonna toss 'em to you 'cause we'll be on our hands and knees lookin' for them in the grass—

Cause I LIKE you to drive. I like watchin' your face in the panel lights. And I can't do that when I'm driving. They got laws against distracted driving now.

Okay, sorry, how about 'cause we're gonna be lookin for a trailhead three towns over, and you'll get hoarse goin' "left, right, stop, back up, watch out," and I'd rather ride shotgun, which I actually wish I had one, if we run into that panther—

Catamount. Not that I'd shoot it, but if he's comin' at me—

I know, they say that about sharks and rattlesnakes, too. And black widows. And snapping turtles.

Maybe. Doesn't make them any less scary. Most of the pictures I've seen, they're not running away.

. . .

So, how far to the next place?

Oh. I told you it's gonna be a long night. What else you got in your bag? Anything edible?

You don't mind? I don't want to—

Cool. Okay. Keep that door cracked, so I can see. Tissue. Plums. Condoms—Whoa, wait a minute, I thought you were—

Right. To hand out. Do the dorm counselor thing. Got it.

What else? Mixed nuts, socket wrenches, wire cutters—hey, a headlamp?

Two? Two headlamps? What the—? We just bushwhacked half a mile in the pitch black, almost lost our clothes, coulda gone in circles, fallen in a booby trap, died in quicksand, drowned—

Let me finish! —and all the time you KNEW you had two LED headlamps back in your pocketbook—

Messenger bag, whatever, BACK IN THE CAR—

So what is GOING ON?

Oh.

I wouldn't have minded. Seeing you, I mean. What, you got some other tattoos I'm not supposed to see? Silver studs, big gold chain hangin' from that lady part I never know what it's called?

Did you get branded?

Well what was it then? I have a right to know, do you have scars or something, I'm not finding you totally honest here—

No. It was fun. I actually enjoyed it.

No I wasn't scared. Well, maybe a little. Were you?

Oh.

Of me? You didn't seem like it.

Oh, well of what then?

In general?

Maybe you have a touch of PTSD. Not your fault. I would too if someone I loved had knocked my teeth out. But—

Hey.

. . .

I'm sorry. Said something wrong again, huh?

. . .

Here.

My mom always said, a little hug goes a long way.

. . .

I'm not your flashback. Okay?

Good. Want a plum?

. . .

Wow—

It's okay. You had your reason. It's none of my business.

I mean it. But, next time, don't let me look in your bag, all right? Guys should know a woman for years before they do that.

. . .

. . .

It's funny, 'cause none of these places is more than a mile or two away, right?

But it seems like they're in the next county, and so many turns, I'd never be able to—

Well, maybe YOU got used to it, but, if I relocate up here, I'll wanna put on a GPS ankle bracelet, with a panic button on it, so they can find me—

Just up here?

Where?

Hey we're back near the college again, aren't we? I can smell the pig shit.

No, I don't. Man, you really are weird.

Hey what's that, it's the moon, the moon's coming up!

Yeah. Wow, I like how you can see the whole outline of that mountain.

No kidding! That's THE Mountain? That whole thing?

Yeah no, totally, I can see that. It's like undulating or something. It's like, you can picture a river running over it, and those are the pools and the rocks, the waves . . .

Yeah, I told you I'm a poet.

. . .

Wow look at the sky behind it.

Yeah it is. It's beautiful.

So, that's the one they're gonna flatten? Where the fuck are we, West Virginia?

They think, well we'll give it a try, see how it looks, we don't like it we can put it all back. Or stick an airport up there. Is that what they're thinking? Do they have any idea?

I think it's sad.

Well, I KNOW those people. I got the payroll stubs. They're a COLONIAL POWER! They got it all figured out. Like I said, they'll either sell the electricity, or sell the company, but NOBODY in the whole fucking county, except maybe the guy who owns the mountain, is gonna go to bed every night thinking, man I am SO GLAD those turbines are up there. My whole way of life is just so much better now—I get that warm glow 'cause I'm helping wean Canada from fossil fuels. Got those pretty red strobe lights all night long like in a sex club—

Yeah, but that's one town. And, it's a drop in the bucket. And, it's in the budget. Paid for by the customers. The rate-payers. Every time some Canadian pushes down the thingee on their toaster oven a quarter of a quarter of a penny goes to the town the turbines are in, so they can hire an artist with a long skirt and a dulcimer to come in and do a residency in the elementary school, sing about the olden days. That's the department I worked

for. A little payola to the folks who own the mountain, and all the rest—

Okay, the TOWN then. And everyone else
in every other town is furious for a while, but it
BLOWS OVER, and then, you've got your New
Normal, and then someone says, well, we got that
done, let's put forty more of them in, flatten out
the rest of the ridge over to the north there, and
all the other—

Oh. What'd I say? It's already planned.

Yeah. FOREVER. And then, eventually, NO-
BODY is left who remembers how it used to be,
well, a few people do, but you have to bend down
near their wheelchairs and wipe their mouth and
listen what they're babbling about—

. . .

Yeah, it's beautiful. You can see the whole dark
part, too.

What do they call that kind of moon?

Waning.

Gibbous?

Cool. What's that mean?

Oh, I could never figure stuff like that out.
Course, women and the moon—you know, you
got this mystical thing going . . .

Yeah? Well, we should hurry up then.

Cause I got class in the morning, and I may
have to shut my eyes sometime tonight. And I'm
with a woman who keeps me in the dark and only
feeds me pemmican.

Whatever. And she's planning something aerobic, you can just tell, and she has the time sense of a Tree Sloth.

Play golf?

When, tomorrow?

Did I say that?

You gonna hold me to everything I say? I told you, 99 percent of it is wrong. Go look at my file.

. . . . .

11

This is it, huh?

Wow.

I mean, wow, I could NEVER, EVER find my way here again. Or back to where we started. I am like totally DEPENDENT on you and we're not even out of the car yet. Actually I may sit here and let you do the hike yourself.

Just kidding. I wouldn't miss this for all the ganja in Vermont.

Yeah, I've hiked a bit. Southern New England.

With company guys. You know, show me what they're buying. Or selling.

. . .

I guess you know you shouldn't drive in any farther when you come to the sign with all the bullet holes.

So, what does "Wildlife Management Area" mean actually? You bring your students out here with clipboards and cameras and GPS, take notes, collect droppings, make sure there's enough alpha wolves around to eat the sick moose, and beavers to keep up the dams so the otters have a kiddie pool to play in, everyone's happy—

Cool.

Yeah no, I'm ready. What do we need?

Check.

Check. Do I get a headlamp?

Thanks. How long is the battery good for?

Sweet. So we could stay out for like two weeks—

No, you're right, I can actually see fine. The waning gibbous.

I promise. Only if I need it. How about we say, only if you turn yours on first.

Good. I am, too. Lead on.

I'm takin' the keys this time. Look, I'm putting them in the left back pocket with the button flap, just in case, you know, I go incommunicado—

. . .

. . .

So far so good. Nice and easy. You come here often?

Me neither. I guess this is a good time to be here though—I mean, if we don't want company, 'cause no one else is around, all your students are home safe, no thanks to you, Ms. Dorm Counselor.

They need a Trojan or a downer or a 9-1-1 call they're totally on their own—

Wow. That far, huh?

I mean, I could holler louder than I ever did in my whole life and nobody would hear.

Yeah, I've never done anything like this.

Mountain climbing at night. You probably have.

Like I said.

. . .

Listen, you can't HEAR anything. Not even a hum. Nothing.

Really? What will they sound like?

Damn. What, all the time?

Swish, thump, swish, thump, swish—

What, more like, SWISH...THUMP...SWISH... THUMP...SWISH...RICKA, RICKA, RICKA, RACKA...needs lubricating... SQUIRT SQUIRT... SWISH SWISH...THUMP THUMP... SWISH... SPLAT!! CHOP!! DRIP DRIP DRIP... one less bald eagle, no great loss, meanest fucking national mascot on the planet. But does it ever stop?

The sound.

Yeah, that makes sense. Duh.

On the other hand once they're up there, you'll sort of WANT to hear the sound, won't you, because if you DON'T hear it, it's 'cause the wind died, and you'll be standing at the kitchen sink, LISTENING for it, lookin' for that flicker on your eyelids, been giving you migraines for the past year, keepin' the kids up, and you'll think well what the fuck did we BUILD them for.

Yeah, every time. Every time they shut off, it's not like people are gonna say, oh dear the wind cut out, well I guess I just won't go on Facebook today, that's okay, my freezer goes out, 400 pounds of mooseburger turns to soup, no big deal, No! They won't let that happen, they'll have to fire up the diesel, or buy nuclear power, or coal. Frack the bejesus out of the Marcellus Shale. That's the Balance Power nobody ever talks about. You have to couple wind with something else dependable, or you're not allowed to build it.

I mean, I still can't believe they're actually doing it.

Real costs, right.

No. People never think about that. Believe me. No one I ever hung out with gave a flying fuck about Real Costs.

Yeah. Run-off, erosion, wildlife, the view—

Right. Watershed deterioration, fishing . . .

Who even knows? Health effects, they're gonna keep doing Health Effects Studies for as long as they can—

Tourists, right.

Yeah, they will. Somewhere else. I sure will. Next time, I want to study environmental writing, I'll go to Lake Pontchartrain. Or Love Canal.

Yeah, freaked out animals everywhere. Crazy insomniac black bears. Hypnotized bats. How do you hypnotize a bat? Snakes tied up in knots. Porcupines hurling themselves at you—

. . .

So, I'm feeling like the path kind of changed underfoot.

And, a little narrower too, right?

Feels kind of like a dry stream bed, or —

A drainage. Neat. Hard writing a song around that, though. "Oh, I'm tripping through the DRAINAGE with the One I Love."

'Scuse me. I didn't hear you stop. Beats crashing into a tree, though.

. . .

. . .

Yeah, I think we do now.

It's darker than I thought. With the leaves hanging over.

And we're in the Green Mountains, so that means, nothin' but trees all the way to the top.

You don't mind, right, I know you're a purist and all. No light, no compass, no T.P.—

Great. Thanks. Just, I wouldn't want to be lost out here all night with you. How would we keep warm?

Whoa! Not right in my eyes, please. Now I really AM blind.

Okay, until they adjust, just turn around and keep on walking and, keep your hands to yourself, please, Miss.

. . .

. . .

You sure you know the way? It's gettin' kind of crumbly underfoot—

So, there's no actual trail then. I kind of thought—

No, you didn't. I'll give you that. You never actually used the word, "trail." So, then, how do you—

Up. Yeah, makes sense. Duh. Up till you can't go up anymore.

Okay. I will. Shhhshh yourself. Why?

What, seriously? We just crossed into their TERRITORY? Aren't you like supposed to make a LOT of noise then? Make them think you're a whole army? Wait, I'm gonna splash more Old Spice on, damn, left it back in my room—I AM A HAPPY WANDERER, ALONG THE MOUNTAIN TRACK—

Right. Shhhhhh.

SHHHHHH.

Ouch. Shhhhhh.

I mean, if the lions are coming back, doesn't that mean the place is all right now? In spite of the windmills? They gotta have other animals to eat, right?

No, I mean FOUR-legged animals.

. . .

. . .

. . .

Sure. Thanks. Water stop.

Yeah. That last bit was hard. Are we ever gonna find the stream bed again, I mean the drainage, or do you just PREFER stinging nettles, prickers, twigs in the eyes, punji sticks?

Right. But shortcuts don't always save time.

. . .

Not quite. I'm gonna go hug a tree first.

Don't worry, I won't.

HEY, point your light the other way.

. . .

Thanks. Yeah, dark chocolate.

Mine, too. It's the only.

So, how much further?

What's up there?

It's not fenced off yet or—

Oh. A little pair of wire cutters'll do that?

Cool.

So, back then when I was ransacking your bag, I think I must have missed the dynamite and fuses and shit. Is there some secret pocket?

Ah. Oh, I got it, in a minute you're gonna give your secret owl hoot, and the rest of the gang'll answer, so then we make a slight course correction, meet up at the pass, secret handshake, I get introduced—

Okay, initiated. Whatever. Is it painful?

Good. What then?

Oh.

We set the charge, light the long fuse, I do a Hayduke, rappel the jeep over the cliff—

What?

I know. I'm kidding.

So, what are we coming up here for? I mean, this isn't like it was at first. Music, draft beer. Wet bodies gleaming in starlight. Toweling off, holding hands—

Point taken. We weren't, officially. I asked you to 'cause I didn't want to get lost—

I mean, I get that the whole night has been one long test, and I'm okay with that, but—

That's fine, your version of fun. But, my version, we're back at Maxine's, my chinos aren't shredded yet, I got a dollar's worth of slow dances startin' up on the box, you have your head right here, I got my fingers on your chainsaw. That was fun, too.

Yeah, in a weird way it was. But this, I don't know—

Of course not. Not a quitter. It's just a bit further, right?

Onward and upward.

. . . . .

12

All right, thanks, I could use a rest.

What, we're here? I don't see anything.

It's funny. Kind of anti-climactic.

Not at all. On the contrary.

This whole night was fated, wasn't it? I didn't used to believe in shit like that. But, obviously I was having some kind of life crisis—

No, I was, I'm not gonna lie; I knew it when I signed up to come here. I needed to do a complete 180. And when that happens you're supposed to meet someone, like, a ferry man or an old leper or guide dog—

Guide Dog.

You're not a DOG. Just, a guide, you need—let me finish—

—a guide, to help get you over to the other

side, I think I knew you were gonna be that the minute I saw you, but what I didn't know—

What?

I'm coming to it. —was, you were following me, you had a whole plan already. You give me little tastes to keep me interested, you—

Like I said, 'cause I work for a power company—

Worked, right.

WORKED for a power company, you thought I could tell you something you didn't know already, that's probably it, you don't DO wind, and power—you do wood and water, but there's other stuff you're not sure of, so you want my opinion, but see, that's where you went wrong, 'cause, I don't have an opinion—you're not SUPPOSED to have one in my line of work, what do you think: corporations are PEOPLE or something?

. . .

Go ahead. I'll shut up.

That was easy. Nice tool.

No, you first.

Are you gonna like, do an occupation?

Yeah. With them.

Oh, so we only have a couple more hours to, like, be alone?

No, that's fine. I look forward to meeting them. Really. If they're anything like you. But, you know, I woulda brought more stuff if I'd known—

I don't know. Change of underpants. Food maybe.

Yeah, I'll bet they will. I'm salivating already. Oatmeal, cold kale burgers and luna bars and stuff—

No, it'll be fine. I'll survive.

. . .

Hey who poured the concrete here?

Wow. Already?

It's some kind of monitoring thing—

Yeah. No, I'll tell you what it monitors, is how much people are willing to tolerate. How do you measure that? That's like what the CIA does in the waterboarding room. SOOOO, let's see how much these guys will take.

Right. A lot.

Well, we're Americans. We need all our gadgets: check. We need to power them all: check; plus, we need to make war and shit on the rest of the world at the same time, so: check. We need the usual thousand times more power than anyone else: check; but this is Vermont, so we got to do it different, lead the way, clean green energy, so, windmills, like a painting by Van Gogh—

Hey how 'bout come here and sit for a minute. Turn the lamps off—

. . .

They're gonna be built, aren't they, there's nothing you and I can fucking do about it, right?

The machines are on the way up? Already on the trailer trucks?

Yeah. See, I knew that.

Right. But still, you have to.

Make a stand. Right?

Cause there's a lot more mountaintops, too, not just this one, and—

That's true. It could be something else. A wetland. Somebody's farm.

Yeah, a wilderness area—

You have to. Just, have to. Whatever you're defending. You never give up. You give up one time, one place, that's when you start losing, big time.

Either that, or you just learn to swallow stuff that used to make you puke—

Exactly, you have to. The long view.

The long long long long LONG view—

. . .

Your hand's cold.

Of course. Do I look like I'm in a hurry?

I told you, I just cancelled all my appointments: writing class, golf, shaving, brushing my teeth, sleep, breakfast—

What?

You do?

You mean right here?

What is this? Occupy with Benefits—Sure!

I'm kidding. But, it's a big thing. We don't have to.

I mean—

Of course I do, who wouldn't, but—

Do we have time? I mean, your friends—aren't we gonna see their headlamps any second? Won't they—

Oh. Didn't see that coming. Just us?

Mmmmm—

Mmmmmmmm—

Me? Of course I'm sure. Been sure for a long time. At least two hours.

Mmmmm.

. . .

Here—

Oh—right. Good idea.

. . .

Wait a sec.

No, I can do it.

. . .

This is—

. . . . .

. . . . .

. . . . .

Oh man.

Wow.

Good thing it's a warm night.

I am. Very.

. . . .

. . . .

Just like that—

. . . .

. . . . . . ! ! ! !

. . . .

. . . . !

. . .

. . .

We didn't have to—

I know. I'm sorry I really am.

No? Then, I'm not either. Not at all.

Maybe we're both a little out of practice?

No, hey, first time is never the best, you got to grow into each other, learn the ropes, hey that's okay, hey—here—

Hey, turn around, look at the view. You can look at me any time.

Yeah, that's what I meant. I meant that. When-ever you want to.

Great. Hey look there's some daylight starting way over there.

. . .

I'm never gonna forget this night. Ever.

It's hard to put into words.

Okay. I read this book once, a novel, this guy almost dies, then he floats all night in a dugout canoe down a river, toward the Amazon, naked, and when the sun comes up he's still floating, still alive, he wakes up, he feels reborn, plus like he's the only human being alive—

No, I don't mean I'd want to be, now. There'd be two of us, that'd be fine. Just need a bigger canoe.

. . .

. . .

Yeah I did. Didn't you notice?

Well, I did. No faking.

I know. No doubt about you. What a voice! The divine Miss M. Still, if I ever invite you to sleep over in my dorm, that could turn out to be a problem.

Involuntary, yeah. Right. Guess it hit that spot Ms. Magazine says doesn't exist. I mean, no *medical* evidence.

Thank *you*. Hey: I have an idea—

How soon is the dark of the moon? It's waning, right?

So. Wouldn't it be great, if this ridge, way up here, now that it's been cleared, is where the mountain lion—

The catamount. Comes up here in the dark of the moon, cat's eyes, night vision, to mark her territory—

Yeah. Like we just did. In a way—

She has a stretch, does her yoga.

Outward Facing Lion, YES!

Yeah, that would be. Let's.

Here, climb off a sec—

I know how to do that. Arch back, cat stretch, curl toes—

Feel the ledge—

Yeah, belly down, fill it up with air, stick out the tongue—

Ooo, big stretch—you need to, after—

Hey I was in the zoo once, in the Big Cat House, this lion was ROARING, you wouldn't believe—kids grabbing their momma's hand it was so freaking loud.

Go ahead, big inbreath, let it out, bring it in, I'll be doing it with you—

OWWWWWWWWWWWWWWWWWWWW—

OWWWWWWWWWWWWWWWWWWWW—

Is that what they sound like?

You think so?

Do it again. Let's see if a real one answers—

OWWWWWWWWWWWWWWWWWWWW—

Nice.

. . .

Whoa—

Did you hear that?

· · ·

. . . a big thanks to Sandra Steingraber,
teacher, survivor, and warrior,
Wildbranch Writers Workshop,
Sterling College, Craftsbury Vermont.
You set this in motion.

THANKS AS WELL to my fellow writer/participants at
Wildbranch 2011, and to the editors of *Orion* Magazine
for running the Workshop so well. To Sterling professor Farley Brown for the hike up Lowell Ridge, and
to the late Horace Strong of Craftsbury Common,
for his informed opinions about ridgeline wind turbines in the Northeast Kingdom. To several helpful
readers along the way: Kate Anderson, Lindy Smalt,
Howard Norman, and Dede Cummings. Gratitude
and love to Mollie Burke, my constant companion, my
eco-conscience.

READING GROUP GUIDE
for
MARLY

1. *Marly* is written in an unusual form. Did it take you a while to "get" this form? Were you initially puzzled—or disturbed—to find the female character's actual voice absent from the dialogue? Was it fun to fill in all the words that she spoke throughout the evening? There is some ambiguity—some potential multiple choices—in some of her speeches. Is that okay? Have you ever read another story written in this form? If you were to write a story this way—that is, one character's words recorded while the other's are imagined—do you think it would be enjoyable to write?

2. Have you ever been in a room, a restaurant, or a train, overhearing someone else's phone call? As the conversation pulled you in (especially if it was loud!), did you find yourself imagining what the person on the other end was saying? That is the real-world model for this particular fictional form.

3. The structure and style of *Marly* could be called cinematic, or theatrical, since there is no description. Without the benefit of descriptive passages, how easy was it to picture the two characters and the places they visited in the course of the evening? How can a writer achieve clarity in a novel form like this? What techniques were employed to do the work that typical description would have done? Do you think that different readers might visualize different images?

4. Something happens with the two characters while they are dancing in the roadhouse. We know the songs they were dancing to: "Mister Heartache," by the Dixie Chicks, and Josh Turner's "I Wouldn't Be a Man." (If you don't know these songs, go check them out on YouTube; buy them from your favorite music source, if you like them.) Meanwhile, think about a transformational moment you may have had that was accompanied by music. Was it a moment of love? Of insight? Inspiration or determination? Does this particular music continue to resonate in your life? If you happen to hear the music now, does the memory come flooding back? Would the moment have turned out different for you if a different tune had been playing?

5. Nonfiction environmental writing is a combination of history, current events, scientific theory, and personal anecdote. Often the writer also has

a point of view which drives the story. Did the opposition and convergence of the two fictional characters' points of view in Marly strike you as authentic? Successful fiction depends upon having reliable narrators: though they did not narrate for you in the traditional way, were the two reliable?

6. Do you think that the relationship between Marly and (*supply name here*) will continue? On what do you base your opinion?

7. Marly is an environmental activist who finds herself in conflict with other environmentalists. She is involved in a passionate campaign to defend the fragile ridgeline ecology of Vermont's fabled Northeast Kingdom. But she is involved in a greater struggle, too: to save civilization from the effects of climate change. Do you agree with her new friend's idea that it's important to take the long, long view in any struggle, that you need to get over defeat, and constantly defend any victory? (Rebecca Solnit popularized this advice in her book, *Hope in the Dark*.) Assuming that you were involved in any activist campaign, how would you counsel your fellows to carry on in the face of an awful defeat? Does a novel like *Marly*, or indeed any form of artistic expression, have a place in this process?

8. *Marly* is a work of fiction. The situation that Marly finds herself in is fictional, but very close to what actually happened in northern Vermont in 2011 and '12. When a writer like Peter Gould

writes fiction based loosely upon current events, does he then become a spokesman for a cause, having to answer angry callers on phone-in radio shows? People may accuse *him* (not his characters) of being anti-wind-energy, and thus on the side of carbon-burning fuels and denying the obvious peril facing the planet. The actual voice of Marly is not heard: is it possible that the voice of the teller is closer to Gould's own opinions? Or, might the author be more sympathetic to Marly's point of view? What do you think? On page 22, *you* have a chance to clearly state Marly's thoughts about the place of ridgeline wind power in our overall green energy future. What words did you put in her mouth?

9. When confronting an inner urge to speak out, have you ever deliberately kept silent? Or, have you decided to speak out and thus face the eventual consequences of your speaking? Public artists— writers, singers, rappers—often find themselves in this situation. In repressive societies, artists automatically self-censor. In societies with a constitutional guarantee of free speech, a person still may decide to keep silent. What are some of the forces that might make an artist decide to look the other way when inspiration comes to call?

10. Please send your comments, questions, and answers to petergouldvt@gmail.com.

If you liked MARLY (and, well, even if you didn't) here are some other provocative books by Peter Gould

Write Naked (FARRAR, STRAUS & GIROUX):

"A great book—has tremendous potential to spread a 'write naked' social movement."
—*The Harry Potter Alliance*

"Eloquently captures the narrow aperture of a teenager's lens on life through two kids with old souls... There's an authenticity in their tentative interactions, philosophical explorations and burgeoning wisdom that celebrates youth in a way that is utterly plausible, subtly breathtaking and a privilege to behold."
—*The Rutland Herald*

"Victor sneaks off with an old typewriter to test out the saying "You have to be naked to write." He expects solitude; instead he meets Rose Anna, a free spirit with an antique fountain pen and a passion to save the planet. Their unexpected encounter marks the beginning of an inspired writing partnership. Together, the teens explore the possibility of connections—to one another, the woods outside, and the world beyond."
—*2009 National Green Earth Book Award*

"Powerful character development and simmering romantic tension build to an emotionally charged yet controlled conclusion."

—*School Library Journal*

"If there is anyone who knows anything about teenagers coming of age, particularly Vermont teenagers, it is Peter Gould."

—*The Hardwick Gazette*

"Hysterically funny, achingly honest, Victor's internal monologue is something that has got to be experienced. . . . With his creating such an amazingly sensitive, innocent, (and terrific big brother) character like Victor, Peter Gould—like his endearing protagonist—is now someone whom I'm dying to know."

—*American Library Association*

"No matter where Peter's going or what he's doing or how far he's moved on the miracle-strewn Peter Gould timeline, he has kept a remarkably open channel for the voices and concerns of real people. And now he's directed his keen skills of observation toward the exploration of what it's like to be 16, with the world unfolding before you, in his beautiful, verdant novel *Write Naked*. Peter has listened to his students, his young actors, his under-twenty-something friends. His ear and heart have heard them, and composed for them this lyrical gem of a book. *Write Naked* is a sensitive, sensual award-winning tale of a boy, a girl, a typewriter, a fountain pen and a cabin in the woods where stripping down to the deepest truth is the norm."

—*Karen Hesse, Newbery Medalist*
& MacArthur Fellow

"Engaging, authentic, yet rich with sensual detail and figurative language. Young adult readers will not want to put down this exceptional novel."
—*Voices of Youth Advocacy*

A Peasant of El Salvador (WHETSTONE BOOKS):

"Magnificent and moving."
—*Pete Seeger*

"Bare-bones brilliant theater."
—*New Age Magazine*

"Teaches us more about politics, economics, and history than a dozen weighty treatises."
—*Senator Bernie Sanders*

"This play is the best way to see with new eyes, to hear with new ears, the struggle of the poor."
—*Henri Nouwen*

"Laced with humor, song, and dance, *Peasant* is a powerful play with a strong political message."
—*The Raleigh Times*

Burnt Toast (ALFRED A. KNOPF):

"Peter Gould must be the Lewis Carroll nightingale of the New Age."
—*The New Republic*

· ·